Enid Blyton's
Do Look Out
NODDY

NOD 1

Illustrated by Edgar Hodges

Purnell

One morning Noddy woke up bright and early. He opened his eyes and saw that the sun was shining.

"What a lovely day!" he chuckled. He stretched and yawned, then he jumped out of bed and got dressed.

"Milko! Milko!" called the milkman as he walked up the garden path. "Hello, Noddy – you're up early this morning."

"It's such a lovely day that I just couldn't stay in bed any longer," said Noddy.

"Now that the weather's fine, everyone in Toyland's going away on holiday," laughed the milkman. "In fact this is my last delivery. I'm taking the family to the seaside."

"The seaside! You are lucky," said Noddy. "You know I think I deserve a holiday too. My goodness that reminds me – Sally Skittle is going on holiday today. I said I'd call for her and her family at half-past nine. If I don't hurry I shall be late and she will miss her train!"

Noddy jumped in to his car and, waving goodbye to the milkman, he sped off down the lane that led towards Sally Skittle's house.

"Hurry, car, hurry!" he shouted.

The car did as it was told and went as fast as it could. It raced along, almost knocked over a lamp-post and nearly bumped

in to Mr Plod, the policeman, who was crossing the road.

"Hey Noddy!" shouted Mr Plod, angrily. "Come back immediately, I want a word with you!"

But Noddy was in too much of a hurry to hear him. He turned up the road that led to Sally Skittle's house, and jammed on his brakes so hard, that his little car almost stood on its bonnet! He hooted loudly – Parp-parp-parp!

Sally Skittle came to the door. Noddy jumped out of the car and ran to get the luggage. "Sorry I'm late," he puffed. "You jump into the front seat, Mrs Skittle. The others can go in the back and hold on to the luggage. What a lot you've got! Look at all those buckets and spades. You'll have lots of fun at the seaside!"

"We're very late, we'll have to hurry," said Sally Skittle,

as they sped away through Toytown. "We mustn't miss the train, Noddy."

"Parp-parp!" hooted the little car as it swerved round each corner on two wheels.

"Ooops! There's Mr Plod again," said Noddy. "Out of the way, Mr Plod, out of the way!"

"Parp-parp!" said the car.

As they raced by, a bucket bounced out of the car and landed upside down on Mr Plod's head. The little Skittles chuckled in delight. Noddy didn't dare stop to pick up the bucket when he saw Mr Plod's astonished face. He just raced down the road.

"NODDY! COME BACK. I'VE GOT SOMETHING TO SAY TO YOU...!" shouted Mr Plod.

But Noddy took no notice at all. His little car swung in to the station-yard just as the train was puffing into the station. All the skittles tumbled out, snatched their luggage, and ran to the train, while Sally Skittle went to buy the tickets.

As he drove out of the station, Noddy remembered that Mr Plod hadn't looked very pleased when the bucket landed on his head, so Noddy decided it would be best not to go near him for the rest of the day as he might get told off!

Toy Village seemed to be empty because everyone had gone away on holiday. Noddy was most surprised to see a very well-dressed toy monkey standing on a street corner, waving a tightly-rolled green umbrella.

"Hi! taxi!" shouted the toy

monkey. Noddy stopped just by him.

"Let me introduce myself," he grinned. "I'm Mr Marvel Monkey, and I go about Toyland selling all kinds of things. I came here hoping to sell some of my goods, but the town seems empty today!"

"Everyone's gone away on holiday," said Noddy. "Do you want a ride to the station too?"

"No thank you, but I would like your help," said the monkey politely. "The bicycle and sidecar I used to travel on broke down yesterday and will take two weeks to be mended. So I wondered if I could hire you to go here, there and everywhere with me?"

"That sounds exciting!" said Noddy. "That would be like a holiday for me, wouldn't it? I've been longing to go away for a holiday like everyone else."

"Of course it would!" said Mr Monkey, smiling broadly. "I know you can drive fast. I saw you almost knock over

that policeman this morning! Ha ha – I did laugh!"

"What sort of things do you sell, Mr Monkey?" asked Noddy. "And where do you want me to take you?"

"Oh – I sell all kinds of things," said Mr Monkey. "And I want to go to all kinds of places – Rocking-Horse Town, Clockwork Clown Village, we'll go all over Toyland!"

"I'll drive you wherever you want to go," said Noddy. "But first I'd better ask my friend Big-Ears the brownie to take the key of my house and look after it for me while I'm away. I don't want any thieves to get in!"

So away went Mr Marvel Monkey and Noddy, down the road, and up the hill, and through the wood. At last they arrived at the Toadstool House.

"Parp-parp-parp!" hooted the car. Big-Ears looked out of his window at once.

"Big-Ears, I've got something exciting to tell you!" said Noddy. "Can I come in for a moment?"

Noddy and Mr Monkey got out of the car and went into Big-Ears' house.

"So pleased to meet you, Mr Big-Ears," said Mr Monkey, and he shook hands with Big-Ears for so

long that the brownie had to drag his hand away. "Any friend of little Noddy is a friend of mine!" he grinned.

"Hm!" said Big-Ears, thoughtfully. "Please sit down. Now, Noddy, what is all this about?"

Noddy told Big-Ears all about Mr Monkey's offer to hire his car to go travelling around Toyland.

"You see, everyone else is on holiday Big-Ears, and this would be a lovely change for me," said Noddy.

Then Noddy remembered that there was something else he had to tell Big-Ears. "Oh yes I think Mr Plod wants to talk to me but I've decided that I don't really want to see him for a while."

"Well you ought to," said Big-Ears. "He probably only wants to tell you something. And what is the name of this monkey? You haven't told me yet."

"It's Mr Marvel Monkey," said Noddy smiling happily.

"What an unusual name!" muttered Big-Ears, staring at Mr Monkey. "Marvel Monkey!"

"It's short for Marvellous," said Mr Monkey, grinning at Big-Ears. "I can do all sorts of marvellous things, like this for instance!" And to Noddy's astonishment, Mr Monkey's tail snatched Big-Ears' red hat off his head!

Noddy laughed loudly, but Big-Ears didn't even smile. He snatched back his hat. "That's not marvellous," he growled. "It's just bad manners! Now go away, please. You're not good for Noddy."

"Oh, but surely it's for Noddy to say if he'll take me round in his car or not," grinned Mr Monkey. "Isn't it, Noddy? This friend of yours seems to be very cross. Shall we go?"

"Yes," said Noddy. "I do so want a holiday. Why don't you come too, Big-Ears!"

"What, away with a complete stranger!" said Big-Ears crossly. "Certainly not. We don't know anything about him. I don't think you ought to go, Noddy."

Mr Monkey stood up, bowed very politely to Big-Ears and walked to the door. "Good-bye," he said. "So pleased to have met you!" and his tail reached out and took Big-Ears' handkerchief out of his pocket!

Noddy followed Mr Monkey, excitedly. He would go with

Mr Monkey, have some fun, and earn a lot of money at the same time! Sometimes Big-Ears could be too sensible!

"Goodbye, Big-Ears," said Noddy, but Big-Ears was very cross and wouldn't even look at him. Noddy shrugged and went to his car.

"Come on, Mr Monkey," he said. "Where do you want to go first?"

"Er – let me see now – to Rocking-Horse Town, I think," said Mr Monkey, settling himself beside Noddy in the car. "I've got some beautiful new horse tails to sell there!"

And away they went. The car bumped through the wood and soon it was speeding down the country lanes of Toyland.

There were all kinds of rocking-horses on the road to Rocking-Horse Town. Mr Monkey greeted them all.

"Hello there! Would you like a brand new tail?" said Mr Monkey waving a tail in the air.

"I'm afraid you won't sell your tails here, Mr Monkey. All the rocking-horses I've seen here have beautiful fine tails," said Noddy.

"Ah well – you never know," said Mr Monkey. "We'll stay here tonight. I have a little tent I put up for myself each night, but I'm afraid it only takes one person."

"It's such nice warm weather, I can easily curl up in a rug on the front seat of my car," said Noddy. "But it isn't evening yet. Let's go round the town."

So they both walked round Rocking-Horse Town for a while and then had a meal in a little cafe. Mr Monkey tried to sell

some tails, but it wasn't any good. All of the rocking-horses had tails of their own.

"Well, well, we can't always be lucky," said Mr Monkey as they strolled back to the tent. "Let's settle down for the night."

"Good-night, Mr Monkey," said Noddy. "We're going to have some fun, aren't we?"

"We certainly are!" said Mr Monkey. "Good-night – sleep well!" and he climbed into his tent. But it was so small that he had to leave his tail out under one side of the tent.

Noddy curled up on the front seat of his little car and pulled the rug up round him. Soon he fell fast asleep and didn't wake up until Mr Monkey tapped him on the shoulder the next morning.

"Wake up Noddy! We're going to be very busy today!" he said smiling mischievously.

Noddy sat up and rubbed his

eyes. Busy? What did Mr Monkey mean? Then, to his surprise, he saw seven rocking-horses staring at him.

"What have you come for?" he asked. The rocking-horses turned their backs on Noddy and neighed loudly. What a surprise! They had no tails!

"They've come to buy new tails," said Mr Monkey. "They must have lost their own tails last night. What a bit of luck for us," he chuckled, and he took seven fine tails from his bag and gave them to Noddy. "Hold each one while I dab the glue on, then fit them to the rocking-horses."

"How did they lose their own tails?" gasped Noddy. "Rocking-horses must be very careless!"

Mr Monkey shrugged and shook his head.

"Who knows! Anyway, it was very lucky for them that we

were here this morning with new tails in our bag! Now then, that will be a shiny coin for each tail, please," said Mr Monkey to each rocking-horse.

When he had collected all the money, Mr Monkey suggested to Noddy that they should next drive on to Clockwork Clown Village.

"Drive off, please, Noddy," he chuckled. "We've both done very well here."

So away they drove. They stopped in Toy Car Town where Mr Monkey bought some breakfast for them both and they ate their breakfast together in the car.

"This really is fun," said Noddy. "Ah, look – there's a sign-post for Clockwork Clown Village! We'll be there soon!"

They drove on and soon reached Clockwork Clown Village.

Toy clowns were everywhere. Their clock-work mechanisms went clickity-click as they ran about. It really was fun to see them turning head-over-heels, or walking round the town on their hands.

When Noddy parked the car in the busy market-place Mr Monkey began to shout. "Keys for sale! Buy one just in case you lose your own! Keys for sale. Bright, new and strong! One for every clown!"

Nobody came to buy. One clown took his key out of his back and waggled it under Mr Monkey's nose.

"We don't lose our keys! I've had mine for fifteen years! You won't find much trade here," said the clown.

"I think he's right, Mr Monkey," said Noddy. "Every clown has a key. We'd better go on to the next village."

"No. We'll stay here for the night," said Mr Monkey. "I want to buy a few things at the market. Besides – you never know what will happen. We might sell a few keys tomorrow!"

They spent an enjoyable day at the market, soon it was time to go to bed again. Mr Monkey put up his tent. Noddy curled up in the front seat of the car and fell asleep at once.

Something woke him in the middle of the night. What was it? Someone was shouting! What was happening! Had Mr Monkey heard it? Noddy peeped round the corner of the little tent in which Mr Monkey slept.

No, Mr Monkey couldn't have heard it, he was still asleep, his long brown tail was sticking out of the tent as usual. Noddy settled down again.

In the morning Mr Monkey folded up his tent, put it in the back of the car with his bag, and Noddy drove out of the little park into the main street.

To Noddy's surprise his red and yellow car was surrounded by clock-work clowns!

"Have you got any keys left?" shouted a big clown with a red hat. "My brother had his key stolen last night! He simply must have another, or he can't be wound up!"

"Both of my friends have had theirs taken!" cried another clown. "So I want two keys please!"

"Dear dear!" said Mr Monkey, in a most surprised voice. "What a good thing we spent the night here!"

"I thought I heard someone shouting in the middle of the night!" said little Noddy.

"We all shouted when we found that our keys had been stolen!" said the first clown. "Hey, Monkey, how

much are your keys?"

"Two shiny coins each," said Mr Monkey, and took some keys out of his bag. "Very cheap!"

"Cheap! Why, they ought to be a penny each!" said a clown fiercely. Mr Monkey at once put his keys back into his bag and locked it up.

"I only sell GOOD keys," he said. "Drive on Noddy!"

"No, wait – wait!" said the clown. "All right – we'll pay. We must have the keys."

Marvel Monkey opened his bag, took out some keys and chuckled with glee. "Who's first then? Form a queue please. Why don't you go for a walk Noddy?" he chuckled as he filled his bag with shiny coins. "I think I'm going to be busy for a while."

Noddy wandered down the street looking in shop windows, and then, as he walked round a corner, he bumped into a small clock-work mouse.

"Do you think Mr Monkey will have a key to fit me? My old one's gone rusty," said the mouse.

"Yes – I'm sure that he will, come with me" smiled Noddy helpfully.

When they reached the market-place Mr Marvel Monkey wasn't there. But his bag was, so Noddy opened it and searched for a small key that would fit the clock-work mouse.

Just at that moment Marvel Monkey returned.

"How DARE you look in my bag!" he shouted angrily. "I'll report you to the police. I won't pay you a penny!"

But Noddy had already opened the bag and when he looked inside he knew something was wrong. In the bag were rocking-horse tails and clock-work keys, a pair of scissors and the fake tail of a monkey.

"Now I understand!" shouted Noddy. "I should have known that you were up to something Marvel Monkey! You crept out each night, cut off all the rocking-horse tails and stole the clock-work clown keys. You left this fake tail sticking out under your tent to make me think you were asleep! Oh you naughty monkey!"

They were soon surrounded by angry clowns and rocking-horses who were demanding their money back.

"You'd better come with me for your own safety!" shouted Noddy as he pushed the monkey in to his car and drove back to Toy Village at top speed.

He drove straight to the police-station and hooted his car horn loudly. PARP-PARP-PARP-PARP-PARP! Mr Plod and Big-Ears came rushing out at once.

Big-Ears pointed at Mr Monkey. "There's the monkey you want, Mr Plod!" he said. "Are you all right Noddy?"

"Yes, but Marvel Monkey is very bad" said Noddy. "I found that out, so I've brought him to Mr Plod – oh, the things he . . ."

"We know everything about him," said Mr Plod, pointing to a poster on the police-station wall. "See, there's his picture. WANTED, MR MARVEL MONKEY. ANYONE GIVING INFORMATION ABOUT THIS RASCAL WILL GET A VERY BIG REWARD."

"I know I shouldn't have gone off with him," said Noddy. "Big-Ears told me not to. But it's a good thing I did, isn't it, because I caught him trying to steal from the toys with his wicked tricks – and I brought him back to you!"

"Yes, things have turned out better than you deserve Noddy," said Mr Plod. "Didn't you hear me shout after you that morning? I wanted you to come and see me."

"Yes, but I was afraid to," said

Noddy. "I thought you were going to tell me off."

"Not at all," said Mr Plod. "You see a lot of people when you're out in your taxi. I heard that Marvel Monkey was coming to town and I wanted to ask you to look out for him."

"I'm sorry, I didn't know," said Noddy. "I promise that I won't do it again."

"Never mind, there's a reward offered for Mr Monkey's capture. It's yours," said Mr Plod, beaming all over his face. "I'll just go and get it for you."

Mr Plod brought out a large bag of shiny coins. "Here you are," he said. "Why don't you spend this on that holiday you wanted? Go and enjoy yourself and send me a postcard as soon as you get to the seaside!"

"Why, there's enough money here for us all to go on holiday," laughed Noddy. "Why don't you come too Mr Plod? That would be so much fun!"

"Well . . . nearly everyone else in Toytown is on holiday so I suppose I could. We could take Marvel Monkey too and teach him to be good," winked Mr Plod. "What do you think Big Ears?"

"Oh . . . all right then Noddy, but only to keep you out of any more mischief," smiled Big-Ears.

"Let's go now then, this very minute!" laughed Noddy. "Quickly! Before you change your minds!"